The Watch Girl

by John Vogt
illustrated by Carol Heyer

HOUGHTON MIFFLIN HARCOURT
School Publishers

Printed in China

ISBN-13: 978-0-547-01767-9
ISBN-10: 0-547-01767-7

13 14 15 16 0940 19 18 17 16
4500569761

Have you ever wanted to be invisible? This story takes place in the future and shows the problems that invisibility might present.

"This is the strangest-looking piece of mail I've ever seen!" said Mr. Penney, staring at a vivid lavender package on the kitchen table.

"Do you think it should be glowing like that?" asked Mrs. Penney doubtfully. "Where in the world did it come from?"

"I don't know," her husband answered. "I've never heard of the place on the return address label. It's from my sister Laqueta, though."

"Laqueta!" Mrs. Penney exclaimed. "We haven't heard from her in years. It's as if she disappeared into thin air! Quick, open the package!"

"I can't—it's addressed to Kendria."

"A package for me?" Kendria asked quietly, from right behind them.

Mr. and Mrs. Penney jumped. "Kendria! Are you eavesdropping again?"

"What's wrong with eavesdropping?" Kendria asked. "I'm just curious about things."

"Curiosity is fine, but no one likes a snoop," her mother answered. "Speaking of curiosity, open your package. It must be a birthday present from your elusive Aunt Laqueta."

The package apparently wanted to open itself because the instant Kendria touched it, a network of thin lines appeared on the surface, and the package cracked open like an egg that had been pecked from the inside. "Happy Birthday" played, and a gleaming gadget was produced.

"How unusual!" exclaimed Mrs. Penney. "It's some sort of bracelet! What do you suppose the numbers 14 and 28 mean?"

"Maybe it's a 'name the pattern' math game," said Kendria. She began to concentrate. "Look, it's a doubling pattern. The next number should be 56!"

"I'm impressed with your math," said her father. "But I think the gadget is just a watch; the *H* and the *M* stand for *hours* and *minutes.*"

"Oh, you're right," said Kendria. "It's a 24-hour clock, so that means it's 2:28 in the afternoon." She put the watch on her wrist. "I wonder what these colored buttons are for?"

"Try reading the directions," Mrs. Penney suggested.

"There aren't any directions," said Kendria.

Just then the doorbell rang. As she went to answer it, Kendria absentmindedly pushed a green button on the side of the watch. A beam of light shot out of the watch. It bent

itself vertically and expanded until it was as tall as Kendria. Then the light widened and neatly swept itself around her like a cocoon around a caterpillar.

Wow! That was weird! thought Kendria, as she opened the front door.

Her friend Maddy was there, holding her baby brother Riley. "Hi, you two!" said Kendria. Riley gurgled and waved his hands around in the air.

"Very funny, Kendria," said Maddy. "Come out from behind the door."

"What are you talking about? I'm right here!" said Kendria.

Maddy said in annoyance, "I don't have time for your spying games! I just wanted to tell you that I can come to your birthday party Saturday. I'll have to bring Riley, though—we couldn't get a babysitter."

"Great! I'll make sure to keep Rocko out of Riley's way." Rocko was Kendria's dog, and the baby loved pulling his tail and tormenting him.

Rocko, hearing his name, came trotting into the room. Riley shouted gleefully and lunged toward him, but Kendria scooped up Rocko protectively.

Maddy looked astonished. "Omigosh! Kendria, how do you do that?"

"Do what?"

Maddy was exasperated. "If you want to pretend you're invisible, go right ahead," she said. "I have to leave now anyway." She flounced off in a huff.

Kendria's mind whirled. How could she be invisible? Then she remembered the light that had enveloped her when she pushed the green button on her watch. Could the watch do more than just tell time? And if green meant *go*, then did red mean *stop?* Kendria had to find out. She rushed back to the kitchen, where her mother and father were still seated at the table.

"Hi, Mom! Hi, Dad!" she said and then pushed the red button on her watch.

Mrs. Penney gasped. "Goodness, child, give me some warning before you appear out of nowhere!"

"Laqueta used to play tricks like that all the time," said Mr. Penney. "Then she went off to be a scientist and disappeared from our lives!"

Kendria dashed off to do some computer research about invisibility. She discovered that scientists were experimenting with things called "metamaterials" to bend light in a way that could cloak objects. Cloaking them in this way made them invisible to others.

It was true then—Kendria *had* been invisible! The watch was clearly some sort of cloaking device!

The next day, Kendria left for school early. When she got to the playground, she pressed the green button on her watch. For a while, she entertained herself by sneaking up behind kids and tapping them on the shoulder. She'd always had fun doing that, but being invisible made the kids' reactions even funnier. But the game lost its appeal when a first grader burst into tears and ran away shouting, "Help! Ghosts!"

At lunchtime, Kendria went through the cafeteria line twice, making herself invisible the second time. But that didn't work out so well, either. When the food server saw a tray floating by, she screamed and flung a banana at it. The banana hit Kendria right on her invisible nose.

Still invisible, Kendria left the lunchroom. She saw Maddy and her other friends, Elena and Lexi, near the drinking fountain. Feeling mischievous again, she snuck up behind them and tapped Lexi on the shoulder.

Lexi looked around and didn't see anyone. "Okay, you got me, Maddy!" she said. "You're almost as sneaky as Kendria."

"That's not a compliment," said Maddy. "Anyway, I didn't touch you!"

"Speaking of Kendria, what did you get her for her birthday?" asked Elena.

"A gift certificate for Bowl-o-Rama," said Lexi.

"A copy of her favorite movie," said Maddy.

"A diary," said Elena. "She can write down everything she overhears when she eavesdrops!"

"I wish she wouldn't do that so much," said Lexi.

"It *is* pretty annoying," admitted Maddy.

"It's not like we keep secrets from her," said Elena.

Lexi changed the subject. "Did you hear the rumor about Kendria's birthday surprise?" she asked. "Her parents may be getting her a karaoke machine!"

Kendria listened to her friends in dismay. So they thought she was sneaky, annoying, and an eavesdropper? Well, she certainly regretted eavesdropping *this* time! Not only had she found out that her friends hated her, but she also knew what all her birthday presents were!

Kendria slunk off and spent the rest of the school day moping. Once, Lexi asked her what was wrong, but Kendria pretended she didn't hear.

Walking home from school, Kendria thought about making herself invisible and sneaking into a movie theater. But what fun would it be to see a movie alone? She tried to cheer herself up by vanishing and picking apples off Mr. Kozick's tree, but the apples tasted bitter.

That night, Kendria couldn't sleep; she kept thinking about what her friends had said about her. She thought about the watch, too. Being invisible hadn't made her very happy so far. Was there a better way to use the watch?

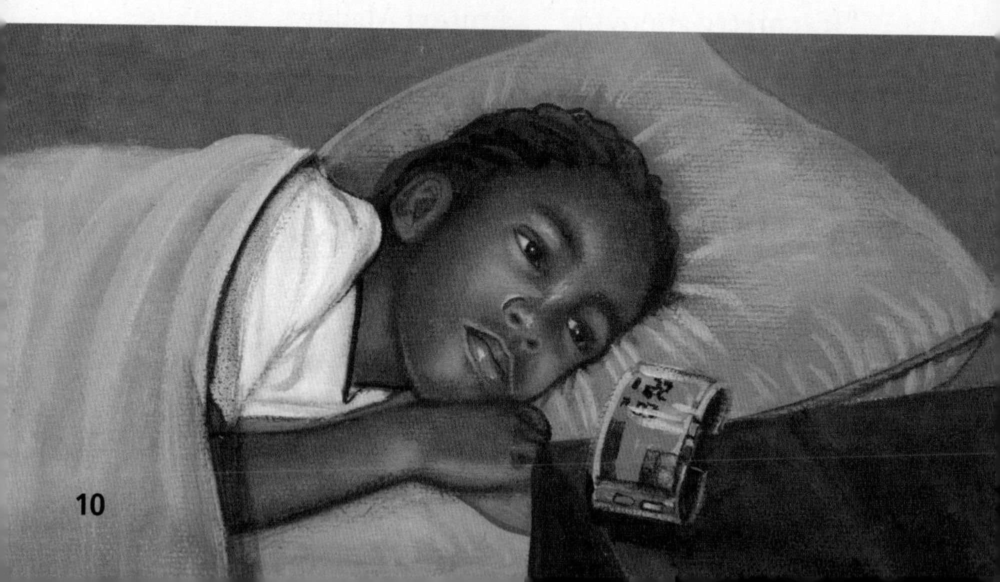

The next morning, Kendria's parents woke her up early. "Happy birthday!" Mrs. Penney said. "We have a present for you, and you can open it now!"

"Here's a hint. You can use it at your party," said Mr. Penney.

Unfortunately, Kendria didn't need the hint. Doing her best to sound excited, she said, "I just can't stand the suspense! Quick! Give it to me!"

Just then, Kendria had a very odd, eerie feeling. It was almost as if someone new were in the room—and that someone was *eavesdropping!*

"Are we alone?" she asked her parents nervously.

"Of course we are!" Mr. Penney said. "Is something wrong, Kendria?"

Kendria tried to stay calm and collected. "No, nothing's wrong," she said and hastily unwrapped the present. "A karaoke machine! I love it!" she cried.

Was it her imagination, or did she hear someone actually *laughing?*

The feeling of being watched continued all morning. Once, when Kendria was putting up party decorations, something very strange happened. One balloon floated through the air and bumped into another balloon. The two balloons then floated off together and joined a third balloon. The three joined a fourth, and the fourth joined a fifth. The balloon bouquet then hovered in the air.

Kendria pushed the green button on her watch and made herself invisible. As she approached the bunch of balloons, it began to move. She tried to snatch the balloons, but they raced away.

Kendria was getting angry. "Stop it, whoever you are! I'm tired of your tricks!"

As if they had heard her, the balloons separated, and one by one, they returned to their original places. "Thank you!" Kendria muttered, and made herself visible again.

At noon, Kendria's friends started arriving. Maddy came first, carrying Riley and a big bag of toys, which she spread out on the floor. Riley ignored the toys and toddled off after Rocko. Elena and Lexi came next, followed by Maddy's cousins, and before long, the house was filled with people. Everyone ate pizza, played games, and sang songs on the karaoke machine.

Later, Lexi and Maddy invited everyone to join in as they sang a karaoke birthday song. Then it was time for presents, and once again, Kendria had to act surprised. “Wow! A gift certificate for Bowl-o-Rama!” she said enthusiastically to Lexi. When she opened Maddy’s present, she cried, “I can’t believe you got me my favorite movie!” Then she opened Elena’s gift. This time, she had to force herself to sound happy when she said, “Thanks for the diary, Elena. I’m sure I’ll use it a lot.”

“Just don’t write too many *secrets* in it,” said a quiet voice in her ear.

Kendria jumped and cried out, “Who said that?”

“Said what?” asked Elena.

Kendria lost her temper. “Someone has been eavesdropping on me all day today!” she shouted. “It’s *really* getting annoying!”

Eavesdropping? Annoying? If lightbulbs actually went on over people’s heads when they figured something out, it would have happened to Kendria right then.

Kendria took a deep breath. "I'm sorry, everyone, I've had eavesdropping on my mind lately," she began. "If I told you why, you'd never believe me! Anyway, I apologize for all the times I've snooped around and eavesdropped. I want you to know that I'll be a 'new Kendria' from today on!"

"We liked the old Kendria just fine," said Lexi.

"But we'll like the new Kendria even better!" predicted Elena with a laugh.

Whatever Maddy was going to say was drowned out by a piercing shriek of joy from Riley. He had flung himself on top of Rocko and was reaching for his tail.

At that moment, Mrs. Penney came in with the lit birthday cake and said, "Time to blow out the candles!"

While everyone's attention was on the cake, Kendria took off her watch and clamped it around Rocko's tail. Pushing the green button, she said, "Scram, Rocko!"

Now that's *a good use of invisibility*, she thought as Rocko disappeared.

When the party was over and the last guest had left, Kendria went to her room to write in her new diary.

"Where's your *watch*dog?" asked a voice from near Kendria's desk.

Kendria put down her diary. "Very funny, Aunt Laqueta! Now please make yourself visible!"

A jovial-looking woman appeared in Kendria's chair. "How'd you know it was me?" she asked.

"I figured there must be more than one watch," said Kendria. "Since you gave me mine, it made sense that you would have one, too!"

"Good thinking," said her aunt, with a wink.

"But why haven't I met you before? My parents told me that you disappeared years ago!"

"Yes, well, I had a little trouble with my watch battery about a decade ago. Unfortunately, I was invisible when it gave out."

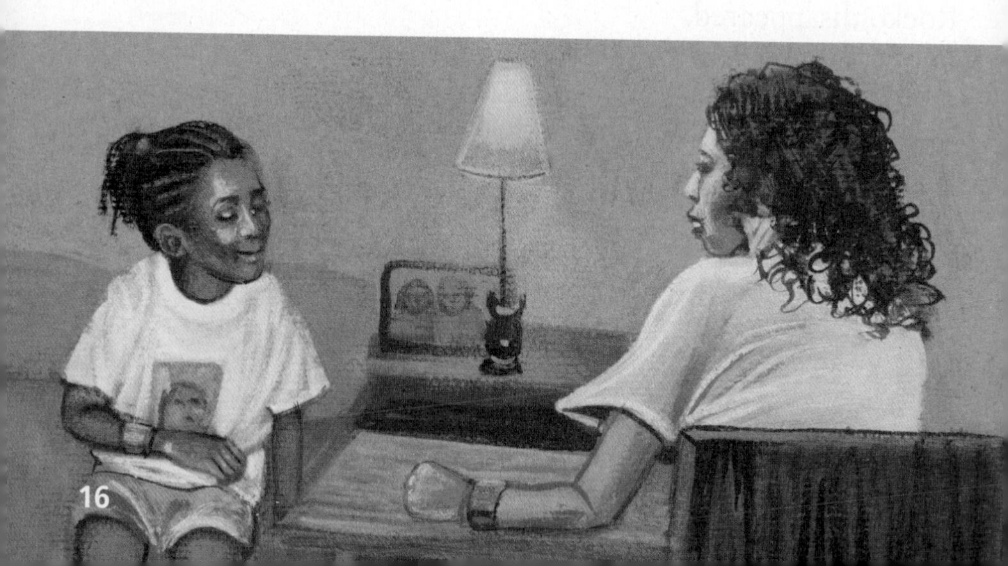

"You've been invisible for ten years?" gasped Kendria.

Laqueta laughed and shook her head. "Not quite. I've been doing a little traveling, too. By the way, I'm sorry I eavesdropped on you. I was just curious about the niece I'd never met!"

"Curiosity *is* good, but no one likes a snoop!" said Kendria. "That's what my mom always says."

"Your mom is right," Laqueta said. "Anyway, there are better ways to use an invisibility watch—like rescuing a dog from a marauding baby!"

Kendria smiled. "I was afraid I wouldn't be able to find Rocko after I made him invisible!" she said. "But then I remembered that he always comes when he hears food being poured into his bowl. All I had to do was fill his bowl and then grab him when I heard him munching!"

"You're a smart girl," said her aunt. "If you ever want to go into my business, I'll be happy to train you!"

"Exactly what business *are* you in, Aunt Laqueta?" asked Kendria.

"I'm afraid that's top secret," answered Laqueta.

"Does it have anything to do with watch-making?" asked Kendria.

"You might say that," answered Laqueta.

Kendria studied her watch. "I know what the red and green buttons do," she said. "But what are the blue and yellow buttons for?"

"It's about *time* you asked that question," said Laqueta. "That's a hint!"

Kendria pressed the blue button on her watch. There was a whirring sound, and a metallic voice said, "Please state your desired destination and year of arrival."

A look of wonder appeared on Kendria's face. "*Time travel!*" she gasped. "Is that even possible?"

"That's for me to know and you to find out!" said Laqueta.

Responding

TARGET SKILL **Story Structure** What is the conflict that must be resolved in *The Watch Girl*? What are the important events? What is the resolution? Copy and complete the chart below.

Conflict	**Events**
Kendria likes to sneak up on people and eavesdrop on them.	Kendria gets an unusual gift in the mail. ?
Resolution ?	

Write About It

Text to World What is the most unusual gift you have heard about? Write several paragraphs describing the gift and explaining what makes it so unusual.

TARGET VOCABULARY

admitted	**impressed**
collected	**original**
compliment	**produced**
concentrate	**rumor**
destination	**suspense**

TARGET SKILL **Story Structure** Examine details about characters, setting, and plot.

TARGET STRATEGY **Infer/Predict** Use text clues to figure out what the author means or what might happen in the future.

GENRE **Science Fiction** is a fantasy story whose plot often depends on scientific ideas.